Where's Dad?

Written by Claire Llewellyn
Illustrated by Cole Roberts

Collins

Who and what is in this story?

Listen and say

Dad

Sid

Boz

Download the audio at www.collins.co.uk/839763

Grandpa

Grandma

🎧 It's morning. Dad is in the car.
Dad says, "Bye! Have a good day!"

Sid gets Grandma's bag.
He says, "Can we go to the shops
this morning, Grandma?"

Grandma says, "Would you like
a toy, Sid?"

Sid says, "No, thank you Grandma.
Let's go to that shop!"

Sid finds lots of things.
He says, "Can I have these, please?"

Grandma says, "Yes, you can!"

Grandpa is making lunch.
But Dad isn't here.

Sid asks, "Where's Dad?"

Sid gives Boz food and water.

After lunch, Grandpa says,
"Here's a box."

Sid makes a bed for Boz.

Sid puts Boz in bed.

He says, "Boz likes his bed."

In the afternoon, Sid and Grandma paint some pictures.

Sid paints a picture of Boz.
Grandpa says, "That's nice, Sid."

Sid isn't happy.
He asks, "Where's Dad?"

Sid and Grandpa play a game.
Sid says, "Where's Dad?"

It's night. Sid is at the window.
Sid asks, "Where's Dad?"

A car.

Sid says, "Dad's here!"

Dad is here!

Sid says, "Oh. Where is it?"

Dad opens the box.

Sid says, "It's here! My new dog! Thank you, Dad!"

Hello to my new dog!

Picture dictionary

Listen and repeat

morning

afternoon

night

lunch

picture

water

window

1 Look and order the story

2 Listen and say

Collins

Published by Collins
An imprint of HarperCollins*Publishers*
Westerhill Road
Bishopbriggs
Glasgow
G64 2QT

HarperCollins*Publishers*
1st Floor, Watermarque Building
Ringsend Road
Dublin 4
Ireland

William Collins' dream of knowledge for all began with the publication of his first book in 1819.

A self-educated mill worker, he not only enriched millions of lives, but also founded a flourishing publishing house. Today, staying true to this spirit, Collins books are packed with inspiration, innovation and practical expertise. They place you at the centre of a world of possibility and give you exactly what you need to explore it.

© HarperCollins*Publishers* Limited 2020

10 9 8 7 6 5 4 3 2

ISBN 978-0-00-839763-0

Collins® and COBUILD® are registered trademarks of HarperCollins*Publishers* Limited

www.collins.co.uk/elt

British Library Cataloguing in Publication Data

A catalogue record for this publication is available from the British Library.

Author: Claire Llewellyn
Illustrator: Cole Roberts (Beehive)
Series editor: Rebecca Adlard
Commissioning editor: Zoë Clarke
Publishing manager: Lisa Todd
Product managers: Jennifer Hall and Caroline Green
In-house editor: Alma Puts Keren
Project manager: Emily Hooton
Editor: Emma Wilkinson
Proofreaders: Natalie Murray and Michael Lamb
Cover designer: Kevin Robbins
Typesetter: 2Hoots Publishing Services Ltd
Audio produced by id audio, London
Reading guide author: Emma Wilkinson
Production controller: Rachel Weaver
Printed and bound by: GPS Group, Slovenia

MIX
Paper from
responsible sources

FSC
www.fsc.org

FSC™ C007454

Download the audio for this book and a reading guide for parents and teachers at www.collins.co.uk/839763